THE TINY LITTLE HOUSE

THE TINY LITTLE HOUSE

ELEANOR CLYMER

DRAWINGS BY
INGRID FETZ

ATHENEUM   *1964*   NEW YORK

Text © 1964 by Eleanor Clymer
Drawings © 1964 by Ingrid Fetz
All rights reserved
Library of Congress catalog
card number 64-19559
Published simultaneously in Canada by
McClelland & Stewart Ltd.
Manufactured in the United States of America
Printed by Reehl Litho, Inc., New York
Bound by H. Wolff, New York
First Edition

FOR LYNN AND KATHY

SQUEEZED in between two big houses, on a city street, stood a tiny little house.

Its little windows were dusty. Its walls had no paint. Its door was locked.

Long ago, it had stood by itself in the middle of a garden. A family had lived in it.

But the city grew up around it. Men came and built a big building on one side of it. They built a big building on the other side. And the little house was squeezed in the middle.

Years passed. The family was gone. The little house stood empty. Nobody lived in it. Nobody cared about it. Nobody wanted it at all.

Nobody but Alice and Jane.

Alice lived in one of the big buildings next door, and Jane lived in the other. They were friends.

On their way to school, they peered through a dusty window.

"Why doesn't someone live in it?" Jane wondered. "It's such a nice little house."

"I guess nobody knows it's here," said Alice.

"Nobody but us," said Jane. "And Mrs. O'Brien."

Mrs. O'Brien was a little old lady who lived next door to Alice. Every day she went out with a basket on her arm. And every day she stopped to look at the little house, just as Alice and Jane did.

They wondered what she had in her basket and why she peered at the little house. But Mrs. O'Brien never told them. She just smiled and hurried away.

And the little house stood empty.

Then one day, when the girls were coming home from school, they saw that the landlord had unlocked the door.

A short fat lady and a short fat man were trying to squeeze themselves inside.

"Look!" said Alice. "Someone is going to live in it!"

But no. The fat lady shook her head.

"This won't do," she said.

"But it's such a nice little house," said the fat husband.

"What use is it when we can't even get inside?" asked the fat wife. "Why, it isn't even big enough for one of us." And they went away.

Again the little house stood empty, until one day two more people came. They were tall and thin. They bent their heads and went inside.

"This won't do," said the tall, thin husband.

"But think how low the rent is," said the tall, thin wife.

"What's the use of low rent when the ceiling is even lower?" asked the husband. "Why, we would knock our heads every time we stood up straight."

And they went away.

At last two people came who were neither fat nor tall.

"This is just right," said the husband. "I can play my fiddle and you can play your harp, and we won't bother anyone."

But the wife shook her head. "Don't you see?" she said. "The fiddle and the harp won't go through the door."

So *they* went away.

The little house grew dustier every day. The mice danced on the floor at night. The dust danced in the sunbeams by day. When lights were lit in the other houses, the windows of the little house were dark.

The man who cleaned next door kept his mops and pails and brooms in it. That was all.

Summer came, and the street was hot. Trucks and cars roared by. Men with drills dug up the street and made clouds of dust and a terrible noise.

Alice and Jane stood in front of the little house.

"If only someone would use it,"

said Jane. "Somebody not too big and not too small."

But who?

"Why not us?" said Alice.

"But it's locked," said Jane, "and we can't get in."

"Let's pretend we can," said Alice. She put her hand on the knob. She turned it, and—the door swung open!

The man who cleaned had forgotten to lock it.

"Let's go in," said Alice. She was brave.

Jane was not so brave. "Can we?" she asked.

"Come on," said Alice

Inside, it was cool and quiet. The noise of the street seemed very far away. They were in a little sitting room. It was empty, except for some mops and pails and brooms. They tiptoed around and saw a little kitchen and a tiny little bedroom.

"It's lovely!" sighed Jane. "If only we could have it!"

"Let's pretend it's ours," said Alice.

But the little house was so dusty!

"Let's clean it up," said Jane.

They got to work. They took the brooms and mops that the cleaning man had left. They swept the floor. They scrubbed the kitchen. They washed the windows.

"That's better," said Alice, at last.

But the little house needed furniture. What could they use? Out in the back yard, they found some boards and boxes. They dragged them inside.

"This box will be the table," said Alice.

"And these can be the chairs," said Jane.

But what for a bed?

"Let's run home and get some things," said Alice. She ran to her house and gathered up some cushions.

"Where are you going with those cushions?" her mother asked

"I'll take good care of them," Alice answered, as she dashed out the door.

Jane took her dolls' dishes and a tablecloth.

"What are you going to do with that tablecloth?" her mother asked.

"I'll bring it back soon," Jane promised.

They put the cushions in the bed-room.

"This can be the bed," Alice said.

They put the tablecloth and the dishes on the table. Then Alice looked out in the back yard again. Someone had thrown away some paper flowers.

"And here is a nice old milk bottle to put them in," she said.

"Now our house looks better," said Jane. "We're ready for company."

Then they looked at each other.

"But it isn't really our house," said Jane. "We can't stay in a house that belongs to someone else."

"I know," said Alice. "We're just pretending."

They felt sad. Pretending is fun, but some time you have to stop.

Just then Alice noticed someone looking through the window. It was Mrs. O'Brien!

"She can be our company," said Alice, and she opened the door.

"How do you do!" she said, as her mother did when company came. "Won't you come in?"

"Thank you," said Mrs. O'Brien. "I was just passing by, and I thought someone had moved into this little house—it looks so clean."

"We're just pretending," Alice explained. "But you may come in and sit down if you like."

"Well, maybe I will," said Mrs. O'Brien. "I've walked a long way, and I *am* tired."

"This is the best chair we have," Alice said. "I'm sorry it has no back."

"These are our dishes," said Jane. "I'm sorry we have nothing to eat."

"Oh, but *I* have," said Mrs. O'Brien. And she opened her basket. It was full of cookies!

There were sugar cookies and chocolate cookies and peanut-butter cookies. They smelled delicious.

"Have some," said Mrs. O'Brien.

"Mm! They're good!" the girls mumbled, with their mouths full of crumbs.

"Have some more," Mrs. O'Brien urged them. "I made them myself."

"But where were you going with your basket full of cookies?" Jane asked.

"I was trying to sell them," Mrs. O'Brien told her. "But I haven't sold very many, and I'm tired of walking."

"I wish we could help you," said Jane.

Suddenly Alice jumped up. "We can! You could use the little house!"

"Use the little house?" Mrs. O'Brien repeated. "What do you mean?"

"You can use it for a shop!"

"Of course!" said Jane.

Alice took some paper and made a sign.

cookies
for SAle
Very Good
ones

She put the sign in the window. Then she spread the cookies out on the tablecloth.

Soon some people came. First there were two boys with a wagon, and then a girl who was minding her little brother.

"Where are the cookies?" they asked.

"Right here, two cents each," said Alice. Then she turned to Mrs. O'Brien. "Is that right?"

"Two cents will be fine," said Mrs. O'Brien.

Soon most of the cookies were gone.

"I see I'll have to make some more," said Mrs. O'Brien.

But then something happened. A big angry man came in. It was the landlord.

"What's going on here?" he demanded in a loud, angry voice. "Who are you, and what are you doing in my house?"

"I'm Mrs. O'Brien," said the old lady. "I live next door." She looked very frightened.

"Well, you can't stay here," said the landlord. "Out! Everybody out!"

"Yes, yes, we were just going," said Mrs. O'Brien, gathering up her things.

The children looked frightened, too—all but Alice. Alice was brave.

"You never use this house," she said. "Nobody wants it. Nobody cares for it. So we made it into a cookie shop!"

"A cookie shop!" said the land-lord. "Well, then you must pay me rent!"

"Oh!" said Alice. She had for-gotten about rent.

But now Mrs. O'Brien felt brave. "Maybe I could pay rent if I could sell some more cookies," she said.

"There is a kitchen," said Jane. "You could make them right here."

"No!" said the landlord.

"Why not?" Alice asked. "I think it's a good idea."

"What if nobody buys the cookies?" the landlord asked. "Then how will Mrs. O'Brien pay her rent?"

Jane felt so scared that she wanted to run away and hide. She was not brave at all, and the man was so big and so angry! But this was no time to hide. Something had to be done. And suddenly she knew what it was. She took a sugar cookie and held it out to him.

"Taste it!" she said.

"Mm!" he said as he chewed.

"Now taste that!" said Jane, holding out a chocolate cookie.

"Mmmm!" said the landlord.

"Now try this kind!" Jane ordered, giving him a peanut-butter cookie.

"MMMMMMMM!" said the landlord. "These are good! Are there any more?"

"They're all gone," said Jane, looking into the basket.

The landlord scratched his chin. He said, "Well—" And then he said, "Hmm!" And then he scratched his chin some more.

Then he said, "Well, all right, you may try it. But save some cookies for me."

"I'll make a special batch just for you," said Mrs. O'Brien. "In fact, I'll start right now. I'll go home and get my pans and flour and butter and everything I need."

"We'll help you," said the boys with the express wagon."

"We'll all help," said Alice.

"You could even live here!" said Jane.

"Could I?" Mrs. O'Brien asked, looking at the landlord.

"Why not?" he said, smiling at her. Somehow when he smiled, he didn't look quite so big; and he certainly didn't look so scary.

And now the little house has someone living in it. At night, when lights are lit in the other houses, its little windows have lights, too.

Its door is painted, and over it is a sign that says:

The Little Cookie Shop

8364